I0581456

PORTRAIT OF A PEDOPHILE

By D. J. Cotten

Copyright © Portrait of a Pedophile By D.J. Cotten
Control Number ISBN
PAPERBACK: 978-1-77419-109-5
HARDCOVER:
Ebook: 978-1-77419-110-1

All rights reserved. No part of this book may be reproduced or transmitted inany form or by any means, electronic or mechanical, including photocopying, recording, or by any information storage and retrieval system, without permission in writing from the copyright owner.

This is a work of fiction. All of the characters, names, incidents, organizations, and dialogue in this novel are either the products of the author's imagination or are used fictitiously.

Print information available on the last page.
Rev. date:
To order additional copies of this book, contact:
Maple Leaf Publishing Inc.
3rd Floor 4915 54 Street Red Deer, Alberta T4N 2G7, Canada
1-(403)-356-0255

CONTENTS

Prologue

The word pedophile comes from the Greek words paido and Phile meaning 'lover of children'. Today, there are many pedophiles circulating in our society. Some of them claim that they cannot help themselves while others though they know that sexually exploiting children is wrong choose not to control their sexual desires but continue exploiting children anyway. The following is although fictitious is a story of one of them. These people for the lack of a better word are sociopaths.

Disclaimer:
If anyone in the following is mentioned either by name, date or place of birth is purely coincidental and the story is totally fictitious.

Chapter 1

It was a chilly, cloudy day in Detroit, Michigan on Saturday, December 28, 1957. In a house on Roxbury Street near Moross Avenue in an upscale neighborhood on Detroit's northeast side lived a family by the name of Hohlfeld. The family consisted of Roger Allen Hohlfeld, forty-seven, his wife Theresa, forty, their older daughter, Barbara, seventeen, Roger Allen, Jr. 'Al', fourteen and Deborah 'Debbie', eight.

That day, Deborah invited her closest friend, Marlene Schreck, seven, over for a sleepover around 5:00 pm and around 7:00, Theresa, Debbie's mother decided to go next door and visit Myrtle, thirty-nine and Grady McAdams, forty-seven and play rummy. Al promised to look after Marlene and Debbie while she was gone.

Al saw his golden opportunity when his mother left the girls alone with him. He had been eying Marlene for some time. Marlene had long brown hair which she wore in a pony tail, somewhat chubby and rather cute with her small eyes and thin eyebrows.

Al was rather slender, 5' 9" tall and had a toothbrush hair cut known in those days as a 'flat top'.

Around 9:00, Debbie and Marlene began their turns at taking baths. Debbie took hers first and after she got out, got dressed and put on her pajamas, then Marlene began taking her bath. After Marlene dried herself off, she stepped out of the bathroom stark naked. Then she noted Al staring at her and she put her hands over her genitals in order to hide them and let out a scream and then she ran back to the bathroom as fast as she could but before she could close the door, Al forced his way in and grabbed her. Then he dragged her to his bedroom and threw her on his bed and then pulled her legs apart and began performing oral sex on her as she pleaded for him to stop. Then Hohlfeld said, "Relax, Marlene. I'm not going to hurt you. It'll only take a minute."

In the meantime, Debbie who heard Marlene's plea, jumped out of bed and frantically ran next door to Myrtle and Grady's house in her pajamas in spite of the cold weather and knocked frantically. Grady opened the door and Debbie rushed in saying, "Mom, Al is raping Marlene. Please come home right away" and along with Myrtle and Grady, Theresa got up and abandoned their game of rummy and Myrtle picked up their son who was at that time seventeen months old. They called him 'Ticky'. He was blond and rather chubby.

They got inside Theresa's house as soon as possible and rushed into Hohlfeld's bedroom just in time as Hohlfeld was getting ready to sodomize Marlene after performing oral sex on her. He just barely penetrated her when Grady pulled him off of her. Then he said, "Myrtle, call the police." There they remained until the police arrived. In the meantime, Theresa felt overwhelmed by guilt for trusting Hohlfeld with the two girls.

Grady was rather heavy set with graying black hair and Myrtle was tall and rather. They were from Harlan, Kentucky. Grady was a truck driver. In 1953 when he heard that General Motors was hiring and paying employees twenty dollars a day, he and Myrtle decided to move to Detroit. Grady hired on at the Cadillac plant in the northeastern part of that city and bought a house next to Hohlfeld's. Not long after, Theresa and Myrtle became good friends and loved playing rummy.

A few minutes later, the police arrived and took Hohlfeld into custody. This was not the first time Hohlfeld ran afoul of the law. Two weeks before on December 12 around 4:00 pm, Hohlfeld attacked another little girl by the name of Shelly Goodenow who was only five years old as she was in her back yard playing with her dog named Spencer. After grabbing her, he dragged her into a garage where he pulled off her pants and began performing oral sex on her and then he penetrated her and reached his orgasm ten minutes later. Then Shelly ran into her house and frantically told her parents what just happened to her. Her father ran out and saw Hohlfeld running away and then called the police. When the police arrived, he told them that her daughter had been raped and he knew who did it. He recognized Hohlfeld as living in a house two blocks away. Then the police went to Hohlfeld's house and apprehended him and brought him to Shelly's house where she positively identified him as her attacker.

The police then notified Hohlfeld's parents and they came over to Shelly's house. Roger Hohlfeld as a lawyer asked, "Did anyone see this attack take place? Is there any evidence of this?" Finally, the police said no and had to turn Hohlfeld loose although they believed Shelly's parents. They already knew Hohlfeld from January 1956 when he was taken into custody for taking pictures of individual girls at school. He spent two weeks at the Wayne County

Juvenile Detention Center located between Forest Avenue and Canfield Avenue on Detroit's near east side.

This time the police took Hohlfeld into custody after attacking Marlene but unfortunately for him, there were four witnesses including his sister Debbie. Then they took Marlene to Ascencion St. John Hospital to examine her. In the meantime, Theresa frantically called Roger who was in Grand Rapids on legal business on behalf of one of his clients and told him what Hohlfeld did and that the police took him into custody and drove him to the police station. Later, Theresa got a ride from Grady to the police station and joined her son. Around 11:00 pm, the police took Hohlfeld to the detention center to have him interned there. The next day at his hearing after finding out what Hohlfeld did, Juvenile Judge Alexander Scott, forty-six, wanted to have him sent to the Michigan State Training School for Boys in Lapeer, Michigan.

After she heard what the judge said, Theresa called Roger and told him since he was an attorney. The next day, Roger went to the detention home to see the judge in order to appeal Hohlfeld's sentence but the judge refused so Roger took it to a higher court. The judges there decided to mull it over and said they'll decide in a few months. In the meantime, Judge Scott was able to keep Hohlfeld in Juvenile Detention until a decision was reached.

The Wayne County Juvenile Detention Center was a terrible place to be in. It was a dark brick building with bars on all the windows and located in a slummy neighborhood between Forest Avenue and Canfield Avenue on Detroit's near east side, ugly by day and sinister by night. It was quite depressing. Hohlfeld didn't mind it since he thought it was worth the price for paying for what he did.

Since the boys and girls were kept in separate departments, Hohlfeld decided to try molesting small boys and he managed to sodomize a seven-year-old. The boy's name was Larry Brosic. When the guards found out, he was placed in one of the "sweatboxes" for a week. That was what they called the penalty box that was used for punishing whoever broke the rules there. At first, Hohlfeld refrained from making homosexual advances toward little boys but started again, this time being careful not to get caught. He almost caught eight-year-old Gary Swanson in one of the bathrooms but one of the guards walked in so he quickly desisted.

In the meantime, Hohlfeld bragged to other detainees how he performed oral sex on Marlene and that was his reason for being there. However, on Monday March, 31 1958, a seventeen-year-old detainee by the name of Floyd Rendell was brought in. He was 5' 9" tall and was of average build. He wore a nylon cap on his head since he had ringworm. Two days later, he heard Hohlfeld bragging about what he did to seven-year-old Marlene and became quite angry over it. Later that day, he caught Hohlfeld in one of the halls and slapped him as hard as he could about four or five times saying, "Listen, _, I have a seven-yead-old sister at home and if some _ creep like you gets hold of her, I'll break his _ neck. Do you get it, _ _? The next time I hear you, I'll kick your _ guts out!" After that, Hohlfeld stopped bragging about what he did.

On Monday, July 7, the judges made their decision in Hohlfeld's favor and three days later, Hohlfeld was transferred to Ypsilanti State Hospital some eight miles south of Ypsilanti and about thirty-five miles west of Detroit in order to be 'evaluated', so to speak.   In the meantime, some of Hohlfeld's neighbors got together and one of them by the name of Rex Marshall, thirty-nine, showed up at Hohlfeld's house and said to Theresa, "We just had a meeting and took up a collection and we decided to ask you and your family to vacate this neighborhood at a financial gain to you, of course, since many of us have little girls too." Theresa simply replied, "Go to hell you _!" and the man left.

As expected, his psychiatrist Dr. Bryant found nothing wrong with him and he was released on Saturday, August 2. Upon finding out about it, Marlene's family decided to move away and did so a month and a half later.

Ypsilanti State Hospital was no country club so to speak but it was far better the Juvenile Detention. It was located just off of US Highway 23 eight miles south of Ypsilanti on the west side. It had three buildings: A, B and C. Those who were there for a short time were housed in A building while those who need long term care were housed in B building and those who were too far gone were housed in C building. The buildings were of yellow brick and the surrounding countryside was for farming. At least it's not as depressing as the neighborhood in Detroit's near east side surrounding the detention home.

The hospital was built in 1931 in order to house the mentally ill and was sold by the Michigan governor in 1990 to Toyota Motors in order to save the state money. Unfortunately, those who were too far gone or no longer had any surviving relatives on the outside were simply turned out and became homeless.

Chapter 2

Al Hohlfeld

In order to explain Hohlfeld's background, we need to start with his parents, Roger and Theresa Hohlfeld.

Roger Hohlfeld was born on August 27, 1910 in Mt. Carmel Hospital on Detroit's west side, the third son of Craig and Barbara Hohlfeld. Craig was a corporate lawyer and Barbara, a housewife. The other two were John, born in 1906 and Edward, born in 1904. He grew up on Cherry Lawn Street, just off of Grand River Avenue. After finishing high school, he entered law school and graduated in 1934. Then he joined a law firm in 1936 which became, Borger, Hohlfeld and Simmons, Attorneys at Law. Roger was of normal height and weight.

Hohlfeld's mother, Theresa Hohlfeld was born Theresa Ann Banks on February 15, 1917, the eldest of two children born to Bernard and Emily Banks. The other was Jeffrey Banks born on July 12, 1919. They had a normal childhood and lived on Mt. Elliot Avenue. After graduating from high school in 1935, she went to Detroit Technical College and majored in criminal justice and graduated two years later. In 1938, she was hired by Borger, Hohlfeld and Simmons where she met Roger for the first time. They began going steady and married in June 1939. On March 15, 1940, they had a daughter and named her Barbara. Then they moved to East Grand Boulevard on Detroit's east side since his job with the law firm was quite lucrative.

A year later in order to avoid being drafted into the Army, Hohlfeld enlisted as an Army attorney handling legal cases especially for soldiers being court martialed. In 1944, he successfully defended one soldier by the name Gary Swanson for killing another soldier. Mistaking him for a German, he was acquitted.

In the meantime, Theresa moved in with her parents on Mt. Elliot and after a year, she went to work for the U.S.O. serving soldiers coffee and doughnuts. In January 1943, she met one soldier by the of Gerald Mapes, twenty-three. After several tries by Mapes, Theresa finally agreed to date him in spite of the fact that she was married with a young child. After hours, they would go to Theresa's house on East Grand Boulevard and have sex while making love.

Theresa was 5' 3" tall, had long black hair, rather chubby which made her figure quite splendid and she attracted many men by it.

Gerald Mapes, on the other hand, was tall and slender and had dark brown hair and was highly intelligent. He was born on October 27, 1919 in the small town of Opp in southern Alabama. The youngest son of Quentin and Mable Mapes. The other was Fred Mapes born on June 18, 1918. He joined the U.S. Army in 1942. Like most southerners he hated blacks so when in June 1943, he was glad to be in Detroit when the race riots took place. In fact, his father was a member of the Ku Klux Klan. He himself shot three black men. Later, when he saw that Theresa was pregnant, he decided to simply ignore her.

As was stated, the affair between him and Theresa went

on for three months, between January and April 1943 when he was transferred to Ft. Custer in southern Michigan. Two weeks later, Theresa came up pregnant. She was quite upset and didn't know how to tell her husband but had to so she wrote him and told him and offered to agree to a divorce. Two weeks later, he wrote back and to her surprise, he said he forgave her since he was still strongly in love with her and she felt quite relieved. Later she wrote him another letter offering to put the baby up for adoption since abortions were illegal in those days. The Roger wrote back saying that rather than putting the baby up for adoption, he asked her to keep it and offered to treat the child as his own. This made Theresa happy so on Friday, December 3, 1943, she had a baby boy and named him Roger Allen Hohlfeld, Jr and took him home to live with her and Barbara with her parents on Mt. Elliot Avenue.

On September 2, 1945, WWII officially ended with Japan signing the terms of unconditional surrender on the U.S.S Missouri in Tokyo Harbor. Shortly thereafter, Roger was discharged from the Army and he joined Theresa and the kids on East Grand Boulevard. As he promised Theresa, he treated Hohlfeld as one of his own. In fact, neither Roger nor Theresa ever told Hohlfeld about his biological father since they never had the heart to do so.

In 1946, Roger Hohlfeld bought a house on Roxbury Street just off Moross Avenue in Detroit's upper class east side. On September 4, 1949, Teresa had her third child and named her Deborah May Hohlfeld. She turned out to be blond and on July 27, 1952, she had her fourth child, William who died only two hours after his birth. After that she had no more children.

When Hohlfeld was about five, he began hunching in bed. Around 2:00 pm on Sunday, April 19, 1953 when his parents and Barbara were out, Hohlfeld took Debbie to his bedroom and told her to undress which she did then he sodomized her for the first time. He did so again a week later. Since she was only three years old, she didn't feel traumatized. Finally, she told mother Teresa who in turn told Hohlfeld, "Please Al, never do such a thing again" and he didn't but beginning the following year when he was ten, he began noticing his mother's splendid figure as most men did at the time.

In fact, on Friday, May 20, 1955, Wayne Becker, forty-nine the real estate agent who sold the Hohlfeld's their house in 1946, came to the door after ascertaining that Theresa was home alone around 1:00 pm.

Wayne Becker drank habitually and he was a regular womanizer. In fact, he was going through his second divorce at that time. His wife Pamela decided that she had enough and she sued for total custody of their three-year-old daughter Barbara. He was 5'9" tall, weighed around 230 lbs. and has salt and pepper hair. He would quite often leave his office Becker & Duncan in Gross Point Woods, a suburb of Detroit and go out for a drink in the middle of the day.

When Theresa opened the door, he said, "Hello, Theresa. Would you care for a drink? I have a bottle of Old Crow bourbon with me." Theresa replied, "No I don't. I only drink socially when I'm with my friends. But thank you anyway." Then Becker pulled out a $20 bill from his wallet and said, "I have twenty dollars here and you can have if you agree to have sex with me." Theresa said, "No, I am married and only have sex with my husband." Then Becker said, "Please Theresa, don't be mad. Forgive me" and then he left.

For Theresa, this was not the first time this had happened and she became quite inured to it so she was not upset but as usual, she told Roger about it. Before that, two other men came to the door with similar propositions. One was a telephone repair man and the other an electrician. Also, it became painfully clear to her that Gerald Mapes only wanted her for her sex.

It was also at this time that Hohlfeld became interested in little girls and he would spend his lunch hour at school hanging out where they played. Then he began to notice one girl in particular. Her name was Paulette McNabb and she was five years old and with her brown hair and brown eyes, she was exceptionally cute. On Wednesday, September 21, 1955, Hohlfeld grabbed her by the arm as she was walking down the hallway and told her that he was not going to hurt her as he held on to her by her arm. She begged him to let her go but he wouldn't. As he was petting her, he felt a slap on the left side of his face. Then he looked up and saw Delila McNabb, thirty-eight, the girl's mother. She was of average build, had black hair and wore eyeglasses. She said, "Let go of my daughter, you _ creep" and he complied. Then she went to the kindergarten teacher and said, "Just what kind of a school are you running here? My daughter was nearly raped by that _ creep (pointing to Hohlfeld)." Then she began yelling obscenities at the teacher and told her that she was taking Paulette out of that school and enroll her in a different one. Then she threatened to call the police. The kindergarten teacher felt bad and later told the principal about Hohlfeld's grabbing five-year-old Paulette and making her mother mad. The principal, Paul Schaeffer, thirty-nine sent for Hohlfeld and when Hohlfeld entered the principal's office, he said to Hohlfeld, "What's this I heard about your grabbing a five-year-old and petting her? I'm not going to tell you again, Hohlfeld, this kind of action is totally unacceptable and the next time it happens, you'll be expelled. Am I understood?" Hohlfeld simply replied, "Yes." After that incident, Hohlfeld just simply looked the girls over.

Sometime later as Christmas was approaching, Theresa asked Hohlfeld, "What would you like for Christmas?" and Hohlfeld replied, "A camera" and Theresa decided to buy him one for Christmas.

After Christmas when classes resumed, Hohlfeld would take the camera to school and take pictures of the girls during the lunch hour while they were playing. One of the teachers, Joseph Yablonski, forty-one caught him one day and said, "Just what do you think you're doing? First, I'm going to report you to the principal and ask him to call the police." Hohlfeld replied, "Please, Mister. I won't do it again" but Yablonski went ahead and reported him to the principal who in turn, called the police. In the meantime, the principal said to Hohlfeld, "I see that you're at it again, Hohlfeld. Maybe the police will take you to the Wayne County Juvenile Detention Center where they might teach you a lesson." After the police arrived at the school, they first took Hohlfeld home and told his mother what he did and then they took both Hohlfeld and his mother to the police station on Mack Avenue and then took both of them to the detention home where they sat before Judge Fred Clark. The judge asked Hohlfeld why he did what he did and Hohlfeld answered, "I just felt like it. I'm sorry. I won't do it again" and the judge said, "We'll give you the forty-cent tour of our facility here and bring you back here." Then they took Hohlfeld through the facility where he saw first-hand how grim it was and then brought him back from the boy's department to the court situated in the middle where his mother awaited him. Thereafter, the judge said, "OK, Hohlfeld, if you agree not to do such a thing again, we'll send you home with your mother. How about it, Hohlfeld?" Hohlfeld simply replied, "Yes sir" and Hohlfeld and his mother were taken home.

The next day, Hohlfeld returned to school only to be

told by the principal that he was expelled. Hohlfeld went home and told his mother who took him to a different school to enroll him there. The day after he was enrolled, he was called into the principal's office where the principal Douglas Dilse, forty-six said to him, "I already know what you did at the other school so don't try anything like that here. If you do, we'll have you prosecuted. Do I make myself clear? Now just go to your class." Principal Dilse was rather slender and wore eyeglasses.

After that, Hohlfeld was careful not to take pictures of little girls at his new school but sometimes he would play hooky and ride his bicycle to different grade schools with his camera to take pictures of little girls while they were outside playing. Finally, on Friday, May 11, 1956 one of the teachers came out and said to Hohlfeld, "Just what do you think you're doing with that camera?" Then Hohlfeld jumped on his bicycle and rode away as fast as he could. In the meantime, a photo developer by the name of Herman Mettler, forty-one, became leery of Hohlfeld after developing the pictures Hohlfeld handed over to him and noticed that they were pictures of little girls, some of them with their dresses pulled up and because Hohlfeld was a minor. Looking up Hohlfeld's address, he called Hohlfeld's mother and told her about it. She just simply brushed it aside and told Mettler, "Boys will be boys and my son is no different."

Later that year at a different school, another teacher caught Hohlfeld in the act. The teacher, Pat Barfield, thirty-five, grabbed Hohlfeld before he could get away and turned him over to the principal who in turn called the police. The officer, Fred Hobbs, thirty-five, recognized Hohlfeld and said, "I see that you're at it again, Hohlfeld. You guys just don't get it." First, they took Hohlfeld home and then took him along with his mother to the police station and then to the juvenile detention facility.

After they arrived, they sat Hohlfeld before Judge Isaac Billingsley, fifty-six who said, "Don't you punks ever learn? I decided to keep you here for a week before sending you home and you're in for a rude awaking" and a duty boy (that's the juvenile equivalent of a trustee) came and took Hohlfeld to the boys department. After the first day, Hohlfeld became used to the place although it was a terrible place to be in.

As was mentioned before, it was a depressing place to be in where homosexual acts were commonplace among the older detainees and there were occasional acts of violence. For instance, a negro detainee who was just as mean as he looked, pulled a fork on a white one just for sitting at the same table with him.

A week later, Theresa came to the facility and took Hohlfeld home. In the meantime, when she was in Hohlfeld's bedroom, she opened the top drawer and saw firsthand the pictures Hohlfeld took of little girls at different schools.

In 1954, Major Thomas Schreck of the U.S. Air Force bought a house on the corner about three houses down from where the Hohlfeld family lived for his own family. The family consisted of Delila McQuade, sixty-one, her two daughters, Madeleine, thirty-one, Thomas' wife and Sylvia Graham, twenty-six. Sylvia's husband was killed during the Korean War (1950-1953) and Madeleine's two children, Marlene, four and Allen, two. Soon Debbie Hohlfeld and Marlene became very close friends. More about the Schrecks later.

Gradually, Marlene caught Hohlfeld's eye and he began to have designs on her but he used his discretion and waited for the right opportunity to get her alone. On Sunday, August 4, 1957, Debbie invited Marlene over to spend the night with her and the family watched the 1933 film King Kong on TV. Fortunately for Marlene, Hohlfeld's parents were home so he did nothing but look her over. Later that night, he hunched in bed over her. Finally, on December 28, his 'golden opportunity' came. After he assaulted her, he spent the next six months in Juvenile Detention before being transferred to Ypsilanti.

After his release, Roger told him, "I had all I could do to keep you out of Lapeer until you reached the age of eighteen and a possible follow up sentence to the state penitentiary in Jackson. Please Al, do control your sex desires." Hohlfeld heeded his father's advice and refrained from attacking little girls

The news of Hohlfeld's release spread throughout the neighborhood like a prairie fire. As mentioned, earlier the neighbors drew up a petition asked the Hohlfeld's to vacate the neighborhood at a financial gain after they took a collection.

Even Hohlfeld's two closest friends, Dennis Hood and Ronald Schwartz no longer wanted to be associated with him, especially Ronald who had a sister about Marlene's age. However, Hohlfeld made another friend in Juvenile Detention by the name of Jerry Greene who was there for a similar offense. They kept in touch even after Hohlfeld left the facility at later met again at the state penitentiary in Jackson.

Marlene herself was quite shaken up over Hohlfeld's release on August 2 so her father came home on furlough and the family began looking for a different place to live outside that neighborhood. They found one located on Woodcrest Street in Grosse Pointe Woods. The family was quite careful not the reveal to any of Hohlfeld's neighbors where they moved to.

During this time, Hohlfeld went to school and did fairly well. However, in August 1961 when Hohlfeld was waiting to go back to high school for his senior year, it came over the national news that the East German

Chancellor decided to build a wall separating East Berlin from West Berlin in order to keep east Germans from defecting to the West. President Kennedy and the NATO allies blamed the Russians for this and told Khrushchev to stop construction of the said wall or else face a showdown with NATO. Khrushchev rightly refused since he did not order the building of the wall. Everyone who listened to the news became somewhat apprehensive. Hohlfeld, who was seventeen at the time, became enthusiastic over it and decided to enlist in the Army. After filling out his questionnaire and passing his exam, the recruiting officer told him that he was ineligible to enlist due to the fact that he was in both Juvenile Detention and Ypsilanti State Hospital. He was bitterly disappointed over this since he wanted to see some action and impress a girl at school by the name of Kim Gilmore, also seventeen. She was of average weight and height for a seventeen-year-old and had reddish brown hair making her quite attractive.

In the meantime, Hohlfeld did notice a science teach by the name of Elaine McKenzie, thirty-six who had a figure similar to his mother's. She was married with two children. She was 5' 4" tall and had dark brown hair and wore eyeglasses.

On Monday, January 15, 1962 around 2:00 pm he caught Elaine alone in the hall and said, "I want to talk to you. Let's go into the anteroom here and chat." Once they both entered, Hohlfeld said, "I'm not going to hurt you so just let me rub up against you." Upon hearing what he just said, she became frantic and started hollering for help. Fortunately for her, a math teacher by the name Henry Denver, forty-two, heard her and rushed in and stopped Hohlfeld. Next, he told another teacher to call the police and Hohlfeld was arrested and since he was already eighteen, he was taken to the Wayne County jail after he was processed at the police station.

At the jail, Hohlfeld was remanded into custody but was allowed to call his father who picked up his mother and showed up an hour and a half later. They asked for Hohlfeld to be released into their custody but to no avail.

After a week in jail, Hohlfeld appeared before Judge Edward Thurston, thirty-six. He was black, of average weight and height, married with three children and fortunately for Hohlfeld, quite lenient. At the trial, Hohlfeld's mother appeared. The judge said, "Hohlfeld, since no one was seriously injured in the incident of which you are charged, I'm going to put you on three years' probation. Now you are free to leave with your mother."

The next day, Hohlfeld returned to high school only to be told that he was expelled. They also put Elaine McKenzie on a three-week leave of absence for her to recover from her experience with him.

Since Hohlfeld was expelled from his own high school for attacking a woman, no other high school would accept him so in order to get his high school degree, he had to take a correspondence course which he finished that fall. Since he was on probation, he had to wait the next two years before being admitted to college.

In the fall of 1965, he enrolled at the University of Michigan in Ann Arbor to study law. However, one of the law professors curtly told Hohlfeld that since he had a conviction on his record, he would never be admitted to the Michigan Bar Association and this hurt him. Thereafter, he decided to study real estate and go into business for himself later on.

While he was in college, he met a girl by the name on Anne Humphrey in 1968. He was twenty-four then and she, twenty. She almost pitch-black hair, 5' 6" tall, of average weight and looked somewhat like the actress Jenifer Jones. She was from Anderson, Indiana. That fall, they began going together.

On Thanksgiving Day, Hohlfeld took Anne to his house to meet his parents and on Christmas Day, after driving down to Anderson, Indiana, Anne took Hohlfeld home to meet her parents, John, forty-eight and Martha Humphrey, forty-seven.

For Mr. And Mrs. Humphrey, there was something about Hohlfeld that was definitely not Kosher but didn't quite know what to do but they kept their feelings hidden for Anne's sake. Shortly after that, Anne and Hohlfeld decided to marry the following June and moved to Grosse Point Shores, Michigan.

On Thursday, May 7, 1970, Anne had her first baby. It was a girl and she named it Theresa after Hohlfeld's mother. Hohlfeld was quite proud to be the father. However, the baby died two days later and this broke Hohlfeld's heart. Most probably had the child lived, Hohlfeld might not have reverted to his old ways such as child molesting but eventually did.

Finally, on Sunday, October 22, 1972 as he drove around as he usually did on Sundays, he noticed a four-year-old girl out playing with her dog. Then he doubled back, parked his car, grabbed her and forced her into his car and drove home where he took her to the basement and started raping her.

In the meantime, Anne was in Church as usual on Sunday afternoons and since Hohlfeld was not religious himself, he simply drove around. He didn't expect Anne to come home so early. When she did, she heard a little girl screaming and pleading for her husband to stop. She was in for a very rude awakening as she opened the basement door and saw first-hand Hohlfeld raping that four-year-old girl. After she got over her initial shock, she promptly called the Grosse Point Shores police and they arrested Hohlfeld on the spot.

After being processed at the police station, Hohlfeld

was taken to the Wayne County Detention Center in downtown Detroit. Since Anne was willing to testify against him, he pleaded no contest. As for the girl, she was taken to Ascension St. John Hospital and required surgery for her injuries.

Hohlfeld was given a five-year prison sentence and was sent to the Michigan State Penitentiary in Jackson, Michigan. He was released on August 21, 1975 for good behavior. In the meantime, Anne sued and got her divorce. However, when Anne caught Hohlfeld red handed, she was five months pregnant. She had a baby boy on October 12, 1973 in Ascension St. John Hospital and decided to put it up for adoption since she no longer wanted anything at all to do with Hohlfeld. The adoption went smoothly. Thereafter, Anne retuned to Anderson, Indiana to live with her parents and began working for Hogan Brothers Real Estate. She remarried nine years later.

In the meantime, Hohlfeld's sister, Barbara married Dennis Mercer, twenty-three in 1962 who was a realtor like her. In 1965, they moved to the tiny community of Quitman, Missouri where his grandfather had a farm and they formed a real estate agency in nearby Maryville. They eventually had two daughters, Diane, born in 1967 and Pamela, born in 1969, They turned out to be healthy happy girls. However, Dennis, knowing Hohlfeld, was very careful to keep the girls away from him.

Hohlfeld, who befriended Jerry Greene in the detention home, decided to write him. By the time Hohlfeld got out of prison, Greene was living with his relatives in Canton, Ohio. Like Hohlfeld, he never changed. After Greene received Hohlfeld's letter, he invited him to come to Canton and help him set up a child pornography ring and Hohlfeld heartily accepted. Soon they began kidnapping small children from various communities not far from Canton, most of them being girls. The illicit business turned out to be quite lucrative but, in those days, child pornography didn't exactly get high priority from law enforcement so Greene and Hohlfeld didn't have much to worry abo ut.

In the meantime, Hohlfeld's other sister, Debbie, graduated from high school in 1967 and went to technical college to study computer science. In college she met a fellow classmate by the name of James Wolonski. Not long after, they began going steady and married in June 1969 shortly after their graduation, the same month Hohlfeld did. Then they were both hired by IBM at the entry level. They moved to a house on Quincy Street on the west side of Detroit. On April 8, 1971, Debbie gave birth to a baby boy and named him Gregory. He had blond hair like his father. They did quite well until the night of June 11, 1976 when they were involved in a serious accident on Grand River Avenue and Joy Road. They were T-Boned by a drunken driver by the name of Eugene Tuttle, forty-three. He was known to be a habitual drunkard. Both James and five-year-old Gregory were killed on the spot and Debbie was taken to Mt. Carmel Hospital with her neck broken. She succumbed to her injury on the morning of June 17, 1976. Hohlfeld, however, did not attend her funeral since he was in Canton, Ohio although the rest of the family was grief stricken.

However, in Canton, Ohio, one of the kidnapped girls, Judy Thornburg, four caught Hohlfeld's eye. She was three feet tall and had red hair. One night, on Sunday, October 30, 1977, Hohlfeld took little Judy for a ride out in the country to a secluded spot and sexually assaulted her. As she was screaming and begging him to stop, he put his hand over her mouth so hard that it broke her neck. She died a few minutes later. At first, Hohlfeld tried to revive her but then realized that she was dead. He said to himself, "Oh my God, I killed her!" Then he drove to a nearby creek where he dumped her body and drove back to Canton. The next day, Hohlfeld called his sister Barbara to see if there was a real estate office nearby and told her that he was interested in moving to Missouri. Later she told her husband Dennis what Hohlfeld said. Later that day, he packed all his things and put them in his car, a 1967 Ford and began the long drive to Quitman, Missouri where Barbara and Dennis lived. Not wanting Hohlfeld to be anywhere near his daughters, he told Hohlfeld of a vacant farmhouse just outside the community of King City, some twenty-six miles northeast of St. Joseph.

In the meantime, back in Ohio, on October 31, 1977, two boys, Paul Zimmerman and Niel Gunn were going fishing, they discovered the body of Judy Thornburg floating in the creek. Paul and Niel ran home to Paul's parents immediately and told them what they found and the parents promptly notified the Stark County Sheriff's office in Canton. They immediately sent out two deputies to investigate. They fished Judy's body out of the creek and took it to the county mortuary and then checked the local missing person's files. Soon they got a hit. On September 28, in nearby Warren in Trumbull County, Raymond and Rose Thornburg reported their four-year-old daughter missing. The Stark County detectives notified the Trumbull County sheriff who in turn asked the Thornburg's to come to Canton to identify Judy's body which they did thus turn a missing person's case into a homicide investigation.

The Stark County detectives launch an investigation into Judy's death and soon went to Jerry Greene's house which was used for the purpose of child pornography. Jerry and his henchmen were very careful to hide the children from the detectives. However, Hohlfeld had already left Canton and the detectives had no idea where he was and neither did Jerry Greene nor Gary Johndro since he was careful not to let them know but he did become a person of interest.

After a three-day drive, Hohlfeld arrived in Quitman where Dennis and Barbara lived. Since Hohlfeld already notified his sister that he was coming, they sent Diane and Pamela to their neighbor's house and then drove Hohlfeld to Marysville to rent an upstairs apartment temporarily. A week later, Dennis told Hohlfeld that he found a place in King City. It was a secluded farm house just east of King City owned by Leroy and Thelma Farber. A month earlier, Leroy suffered a stroke and could no longer manage the farm so they moved in with their son in St. Joseph. Since Dennis couldn't sell the farm, he decided to rent it out to Hohlfeld in order to keep him away from his young daughters. Hohlfeld took a job at a Gerbes supermarket in nearby Bethany as a stocker. He made new friends there a would go out at a local bar for drinks. Not long after, he would drive around to various towns where he was totally unknown to the people, looking for little girls to prey on. Since Hohlfeld was bankrolled by his father, money was no problem for him.

Finally, on Sunday, June 11, 1978, he found one while driving through the small town of Gower, some twenty miles southeast of St. Joseph, by the name of Diana Fee, seven. As he saw her outside playing with other children, he suddenly grabbed her and once inside his car, he blindfolded her and tied her hands with duct tape and then drove to a secluded spot in the countryside and sexually assaulted her and fearing to become a person of interest, he drove Diana back to Gower and turned her loose near where she lived and promptly drove off. Upon hearing what happened to Diana, the townspeople became terrified, especially her parents, Gabriel, Forty-one and Loretta Fee, thirty-nine. Gabriel was an itinerant musician and Loretta, a local factory worker.

After raping Diana, Hohlfeld decided to lay low for a month but on Friday, July 21, as he was driving through Maysville in DeKalb County, he found an eight-year-old girl by the name of Connie White. She was blonde and lived in a trailer just west of Maysville. He followed her to her trailer where she lived with her parents, Ruth, fort-three and Larry White, fifty. Two days later, he returned and grabbed Connie and like Diana, he blindfolded her and tied her hands with duct tape. After sexually assaulting her, he drove her to the vicinity of where she lived and promptly drove off.

On Friday, July 28 around 4:30 pm as he was drinking a beer in a tavern in Stanberry, he suddenly noticed a girl walking by. She was dressed in blue shorts and a white blouse that was tied, exposing her belly navel and she was extremely pretty. She had dark brown kinky hair that she wore done up in a bun and brown eyes. Her name was Judy Shaan and she was eleven years old.

Upon seeing her, Hohlfeld got up and ran outside to his car to follow her. More on Judy Shaan later.

Chapter 3

Marlene Schreck was born on the Ramstein Air Force Base in the Rhineland-Palatinate on June 24, 1950 to Airman Thomas, twenty-seven and Madeleine Schreck, twenty-three. On January 31, 1952, they had their second child, a boy which they named Allen George. Thomas enlisted in the Army in 1942 after finishing high school in order to avoid being drafted and he opted for the Army Air Force. He grew up on Cherry Lawn Street just off of Grand River Avenue on the west side of Detroit. He had a normal childhood growing up with his older brother Wilbur and his younger sister, Jennifer. Madeleine, on the other hand, was born Madeleine McQuade on January 25, 1927 and grew up on Hilger Street on Detroit's east side. Like Thomas, she had an older brother named Quincy, born in 1920 and a younger sister named Sylvia, born in 1931, Madeleine's parents finally bought a house on Dickerson Street in 1938 in a middle-class neighborhood.

After the war, Thomas decided to remain in the Army Air Force due to his love of flying. In March 1947 while on furlough, Thomas met Madeleine at dance at a USO branch on Jefferson Avenue, not far from where Madeleine lived.

Thereafter, they began going steady and finally married that June.

In the meantime, back in Europe in 1948, the Russians decided to grant East Germany its independence and unite West Berlin with East Berlin thus creating a united city under Communist rule. In order to accomplish this, the Russians decided to cut off West Berlin from the allied occupied part of Germany so they closed all roads connecting the two hoping to starve West Berlin into submission. The allies then decided to organize an airlift into West Berlin supplying the West Berliners with food and fuel. It was known as the Big Lift beginning in June 1948 and ending in May 1949. It eventually succeeded.

Seeing that more pilots were needed for this operation, Thomas was deployed to Ramstein Air Force base in the Rhein valley where he was to take part in the Big Lift. Madeleine went with him and lived on the base. It was here where both Marlene and her brother Allen were born.

In 1952, Thomas decided that he didn't want the kids to grow up in Germany where they didn't know the language or the customs so he took Madeleine and the kids to her mother's place on Dickerson Street. In the meantime, Madeleine's father, Elmer McQuade died in 1946 from cardiac failure and her sister, Sylvia married her high school sweetheart, Hugh Graham in 1949 upon graduating. Both were in the same grade. In 1951, Hugh was drafted into the U.S. Army and later sent to Japan. Sylvia followed him there in order to be near him. On June 25, 1950, war broke out in Korea.

Early in 1952, Hugh was deployed in Korea but was killed in combat on April 9. Soon after, Sylvia left Japan and went back to Detroit to live with her mother Delila. Sylvia was rather slender and had brown hair and looked a little like Marlene.

In 1954, having risen to the rank of Air Force major,

Thomas decided that Madeleine's family deserved to live in an upscale neighborhood instead of the middle class one on Dickerson Street so while of furlough, he bought a house on Roxbury Street just off of Moross Road just three houses down from where the Hohlfeld's lived.

A year later when both Debbie Hohlfeld and Marlene were old enough to attend kindergarten, the two became close friends. Unfortunately, Hohlfeld began having signs on Marlene but never got her alone with him until his 'golden opportunity' came. In the meantime, he continued taking his camera with him to different elementary schools taking pictures of little girls.

Finally, on December 28, 1957, his golden opportunity came but he was later arrested and sent to Juvenile Detention where he spent the next six months before being transferred to Ypsilanti where he only stayed for only three weeks.

That night after Marlene was sexually assaulted by Hohlfeld, she was taken to Ascension St. John Hospital and treated although Hohlfeld hardly got a chance to penetrate her. When Marlene's family learned of Hohlfeld's release from Ypsilanti, they became horrified for Marlene's sake so they decided to move away. Not long after, they found a house in Grosse Pointe Woods and moved there. Shortly thereafter on November 4, she was sent to a place called Hawthorn Center in Livonia, a suburb northwest of Detroit. After she was sent home on April 23, 1959, she was being counseled by a Wayne County social worker by the name of Edith Mize, thirty-one a week later. Edith, like Marlene's aunt Sylvia, had a husband who was killed in combat in Korea. She was born on Edith Lawrence May 8, 1928 in Mt. Carmal Hospital on Detroit's west side. She had two brothers both older than her. One day in the spring of 1940, she was sexually assaulted in a wooded area by three teenage boys and left traumatized. She was some 5' 8" tall, had red hair and had a very voluptuous figure. It took her a very long time to get over what those boys did to her but she finally succeeded and married Seth Mize on January 28, 1950. He was drafted later that year and deployed to Japan and shortly after that she move there in order to be near him.

On Friday, June 12, 1959, Sylvia remarried a man by the name of James Hubbard and they soon got a place of their own on Chandler Park Drive. They eventually had four children.

After being counselled by Edith, Marlene gradually got over her fear of boys just as Edith did. In 1965 when she was fifteen, she began dating but was careful not to deceive whoever she dated by admitting what happened to her when she was seven. At that time, she decided that she wanted to become a nurse in order to help people just as Edith helped her.

In 1968, when she was eighteen, she graduated from high school and enrolled in Eastern Michigan University in Ypsilanti, Michigan. That summer while she was waiting to attend classes that fall, she hired on at Buxton and Skinner Press, Inc. on Gratiot Avenue. After she was hired, she went to work on the 4:00 pm to the 12:00 am shift. While she was working there, she met a machine operator by the name of James Warren Smith, twenty-five. He was 5' 9" tall, had kinky brown hair and rough looking. He also had a hateful demeanor and a terrible temper so most of his coworkers were afraid of him. They called him 'J.W.'.

J.W. was born James Warren Smith on February 17, 1943 in Mt. Carmel Hospital on the west side of Detroit to Robert and Emily Smith. J.W. was an only child. When J.W. was born, his father was in the Army stationed in Europe and later took part in the D-day invasion of France on June 6, 1944. After his discharge, he went back to work for Chrysler Motors at their DeSoto plant. Even in school,

J.W. became aggressive and pushed other students around often getting into fights. In high school, he was suspended so many times that he didn't graduate until 1962 when he was already nineteen. Shortly after that, he was drafted into the Army and served two years until he was discharged in 1964. First, he went to work for Chrysler Motors but a year later, he found out that Buxton and Skinner paid more in the long run so he went to work for them eventually becoming an operator.

He became attracted to Marlene and she felt the same way about him. After the first two weeks, J.W. asked her out for a date and she readily agreed. Soon they started going steady but as in the case of most men she dated, she decided to tell him what happened to her when she was seven. One night while they were out on a date she opened up and said, "J.W, there's something I must tell you about me before we go any farther. J.W., when I was seven, I was sexually assaulted by a fourteen-year-old boy. He was the brother of my friend Debbie. His mother trusted him to look after us while she went next door to visit her friends. Then he took advantage of her absence to assault me by performing oral sex. He would have sodomized me had she and her friends not pulled him off of me. The police arrested him and they took me to the hospital. Oh J.W., I'm so sorry to tell you this but it would be so unfair to you not to. Please J.W., try to forgive me if you can."

J.W.'s reaction was not at all what she expected from him. Instead of deciding to drop Marlene, he became quite indignant and said, "Who is the _ creep who did this to you? I Want to break his _ back! All you have to do Honey is to name him and tell me where he lives." Marlene replied, "No, J.W. I won't do that." Then J.W. said, "Why on God's green earth are you protecting this _ _ who did it to you?" Marlene replied, "No, J.W. It's not him I'm protecting, it's you! Judging by your demeanor, I know once you find out who he is and where he lives, you'll go after him and maybe injure him and the police will arrest you for battery and throw you in jail. That I do not want! Besides, that was more than ten years ago. Please J.W., try to get over it like I did." Then J.W. said, "Please, Marlene, come to think of it, you're probably right but it's so hard to swallow right now."

After three or four days, J.W. gradually calmed down over what Marlene told him and in fact, it somehow caused him to love her more than before and Marlene to her surprise, loved him more than ever. However, as September was approaching and her fall classes were about to start, J.W. asked her not to go to Ypsilanti but continue working at Buxton & Skinner instead, she replied, "No, J.W., since I was assaulted as a child, I always wanted to help others and I can do that by being a nurse." J.W. replied, "Marlene, you can make more money here by building up your seniority and becoming an operator." Then Marlene said, "I can but that will keep me from helping other people the way I was helped by Mrs. Mize." J. W. replied, "What about us? It's a long way to Ypsilanti." Then Marlene said, "We can still see one another on weekends. I have my '58 Chevy and you your 1966 Dodge." Upon graduating from high school, Marlene's parents bought her a blue 1958 Chevrolet and it looked almost brand new.

For Marlene, college tuition was no problem since her uncle Wilbur Schreck, forty-seven, offered to pay. Wilbur was a lifelong bachelor who doted on Marlene. He was the brother of Thomas Schreck and a college professor who taught journalism at the Wayne County technical college.

About two days before Christmas when J. W. was visiting relatives and not expected back for about three days, a hoodlum by the name of Ernie Beatty decided to make his move and hit on Marlene by going up to her apartment with a bouquet and said he wanted to date her, Marlene said, "No, I don't want to go anywhere with you and besides,

I already have a boyfriend so please leave." Ernie replied, "Where is he? I don't see him." Then unexpectedly, J. W. showed up and said, "Listen, __ that's my girl you're _ with. If I ever see you anywhere near her or hear about it, I'll kick your _ guts out! Do you get my drift? Now get the _ out of here." Ernie was only 5' 4" tall and weighed around 135 lbs. He was twenty-six.

Marlene said, "Please, J. W., he just showed up out of the blue. Don't do anything to hurt him." J.W. replied, "No Marlene, I won't this time but if he comes back, I will."

Finally, in June 1970, Marlene graduated with an associate degree in medicine and was soon hired on at Mt. Carmel Hospital on Detroit's west side. In the meantime, Marlene and J. W. were married. On Monday, May 10, 1971, Marlene had her first baby and named him Gabriel.

As for Marlene's brother Allen, he joined the Air Force after graduating from high school the same month Marlene did from college. Two years later, Marlene's father, Thomas retired and came home.

Chapter 4

Hohlfeld blinded, arrested and jailed

As was mentioned before, on Friday, July 28, 1978 around 4:00 pm while he was drinking a beer in Mrs. Connelley's tavern in Stanberry, Hohlfeld noticed a girl walking by, dressed in a white blouse and green shorts and that she was extremely pretty for an eleven-year-old girl. She had brown hair which she wore in a bun and brown eyes and her blouse was tied up thus exposing her belly navel and a birthmark below on the left side. She did look somewhat like Marlene Schreck. Upon seeing her, Hohlfeld suddenly got up and ran outside to his blue 1974 Ford Mustang, got in and followed her but being careful not to let her notice.

The girl that attracted Hohlfeld's attention was named Judy Schaan and as mentioned earlier was quite attractive. She was born Judith Gail Schaan on September 24, 1966, the oldest child of Eric, thirty-nine and Louisa Shaan, thirty-seven in St. Joseph Medical Center just north of Albany, Missouri. The others were Frederick George Schaan born on January 31, 1969 followed by Patricia Ulrika born on March 10, 1975. Eric taught general science and math at Stanberry High School and Louisa, a housewife. Eric was from the nearby community of Savanna, Missouri and Louisa was born in 1941 in the German village of Quakenbruck. After graduating from the University of Missouri in Kansas City in 1963 with a master's degree in genral science, Eric was drafted into the Army and served his second tour of duty in West Germany where he met Louisa Muenks. Toward the end of his tour in 1965, they married so Louisa could come with him to America as his wife. After his return, Eric applied for a teacher's job in his hometown of Savanna but as there were no vacancies there, he was informed that that there was an opening in nearby Stanberry and he applied for it and was accepted. The couple moved there and lived there ever since.

Judy was quite popular in school and with her beauty and charisma, other classmates, not only the girls but most of the boys tended to gravitate toward her. Her two best friends were Naomi Grant and Phyllis Magruder. Naomi had red hair and of average size for twelve-year-old and Phyllis was a blond. All three had a passion for bowling and horseback riding and went to the Silver Saddle Bowling and Lounge on most Saturday afternoons.

That weekend Hohlfeld could not get his mind off Judy. On Sunday, Hohlfeld drove east to Hamilton and spent the night in a motel just east of that town. The next day as Hohlfeld was driving around, he spotted a three-year-old red headed girl by the name of Danielle Callan playing with other kids near where she lived. After he drove by, he made a u turn and doubled back. Then he grabbed her, took to a secluded place and sodomized her after performing oral sex on her and then took her back to where he grabbed her.

After he dropped her off near where he grabbed her, the other kids went to tell her parents, Fred, forty-seven and Delila Callan, forty-five. Both parents were devastated by what happened to her. Then they realized that there was a serial child rapist running around. She was so injured by the rape Hohlfeld perpetrated on her that she required surgery and the Caldwell Sheriff's department was notified. Shortly after he raped Danielle, Hohlfeld drove back to King City, far from Hamilton. Unfortunately, none of the children who witnessed Danielle's kidnapping could describe Hohlfeld or his car.

In the meantime, Hohlfeld still could not get his mind off Judy whom he spotted that Friday so he drove again to Stanberry without seeing her but finally on Saturday, August 5, he did spot her with her friends leaving the Silver Saddle and followed her to where she lived without letting her know it. This way, he got her address which was 25 Quincy Street on Stanberry's west side.

He would drive to Stanberry to follow her and find out when she would go out with her friends but couldn't find her alone. That following Monday, one of her friends, Phyllis said to her, "Judy, did you notice that man in a blue Ford Mustang? Lately, he seemed to be going everywhere we go. He's beginning to give me the creeps but it probably doesn't mean anything." Then around 8:30 pm on Tuesday, August 8, as they were out riding their bicycles on the way to Judy's house, Naomi said, "There he is again, Judy. That man in the blue Mustang seems to be interested in you. Be careful, like Phyllis, he's giving me the creeps."

After that, Judy began to feel uneasy so she took the scissors she used to trim plants in the garden and put them in her pocket. Her parents began to notice this change in her and she finally told them what made her so uneasy and they understood.

Finally. On Saturday, August 12, around 10:00 am, Hohlfeld decided to make his move so he parked his car about two houses down from where she lived and waited for her to come out. About an hour later, she did and hopped on her bike. Then Hohlfeld got out of his car and approached her saying, "Young lady, I lost my dog so can you help me find him?" Judy realized at once that it was the same man who had singled her out among her friends and been stalking her. At first, she was seized by fear and then the anger kicked in. When she told him no and wanted to meet her friends, he grabbed her, pulled her off her bike and put his hand over her mouth so she couldn't scream and then a Labrador Golden Retriever, the family dog ran up to them and began barking at Hohlfeld and biting him on the leg. Hohlfeld took his hand from Judy's mouth to shoo him away. Taking advantage of this, Judy reached into her pocket and pulled out her scissors and jabbed Hohlfeld in his right eye then as he took his other hand off of her and covered his eye, Judy then jabbed him in his left eye leaving him totally blind.

The neighbor next door, a widow, Mrs. Edwina Belle, ninety-two, having finished her breakfast, looked out her window and saw what was going on and she was shocked. Having covered his face with both hands with blood gushing out, Hohlfeld began yelling obscenities at Judy, hollering things like, "You _ _, you _ _" and other obscenities. Judy ran back to her house and told her parents what took place. Eric was about to call the Gentry County Sheriff's department when he noticed that someone already had. Two deputies, Kevin Caruthers, forty-one and Dan Hurley, forty-seven showed up. First, they noticed Hohlfeld with his hands over his face with blood gushing out and covering his arms and shirt yelling obscenities at Judy. Then the deputies called for an ambulance to take Hohlfeld to the St. Joseph Medical Center to be treated. He was so shaken up that the paramedics had to give him a double dose of Thorazine to calm him down. Then Eric took Judy by the hand and went outside with her. Then Judy said to her father, "Dad, I need to tell the deputies what I did" and she approached one of the deputies and said, "Officer, I jabbed his eyes out as he was dragging me toward his car, that blue Ford Mustang over there. I'm ready to be punished for what I did. Here are my scissors." Then Eric intervened and said, "I'm Eric Shaan, Judy's father. I need to go with her if you take her in." Deputy Hurley replied, "No, Mr. Shaan, that won't be necessary now as we're still investigating what's happened here. Then we'll get back to you." Then Eric took Judy home.

Then Mrs. Belle came out and approached the deputies saying, "Deputies, I saw the whole thing taking place. That man over there with the blood on his face grabbed Judy and started dragging her then their Labrador Retriever run up to that man barking and tried to bite him as he tried to shoo it away. Then Judy took out her scissors and stabbed him. Please officers, don't do anything to Judy. That man meant to hurt her."

Upon hearing what happened in Stanberry, Sheriff Dan Abbott, forty-nine of Gentry County called both Sheriff Francis Corrigan, seventy-four of DeKalb County and Sheriff Robert Harrington, fifty-three of Clinton County telling them that they found a suspect of Connie White, eight, and Diana Fee, seven cases respectively. Both girls were taken to the St. Joseph Medical Center and both positively Hohlfeld as their assailant later that day.

In the meantime, after injecting Hohlfeld with Thorazine, the paramedics took him to the hospital with his face covered with a towel. Upon concluding their investigation, one of the deputies went to Judy's house around 7:30 pm to notify her parents saying, "Your daughter did what she had to in order to save herself. We have ascertained that the man who tried to abduct her this morning had raped two other girls lately."

At first, Judy felt remorse over what she did but later became angry over the fact that he had her singled out from among her friends and had sinister plans for her.

In the hospital still under sedation, he was notified that he was being placed under arrest, not only for trying to kidnap Judy but for the kidnapping and rape of two other girls as well after he was read his rights not to tell them anything without his attorney present. Then they told Hohlfeld that he was entitled to make one phone call. Later that day, Jerry Slocum, thirty-one, was appointed his attorney. Then Slocum went to see the county prosecutor Zack Thorpe, fifty-seven, in order to find out the evidence he had against Hohlfeld. Thorpe said, "With all the evidence we have here, it would be better if your client took a plea and Slocum agreed. Around 6:30 pm, Slocum went to the hospital and told Hohlfeld the news he got from Thorpe. Hohlfeld simply said, "What the hell, there's nothing they can do to hurt me now."

After the deputies left, Hohlfeld made his phone call to his sister Barbara in Quitman. Since he was blind, one of the nurses had to dial for him. Hohlfeld said to his sister after she picked up the phone, "Barbara, I'm in a hospital in Albany, blind as a bat. I can't see anything now. Some _ _ grabbed a pair of scissors and jabbed my eyes out." Barbara, not surprised, replied, "Did you try to rape her, Al?" I bet you did. I know you and you never changed. Now I'm going to call Mom and tell her about what happened to you."

In October 1975, shortly after Hohlfeld's release from the Michigan state penitentiary in Jackson, Michigan, Roger and Theresa bought a new house in the Detroit suburb of Sterling Heights, near Utica, north of Detroit. Hohlfeld decided to move to Canton, Ohio to join his new friends, Jerry Greene and Gary Johndro.

In early 1978, Roger began to show early signs of Alzheimer's disease so he finally went to see his doctor Roger Phelps on October 12 of that year. After several tests, it was confirmed that Roger did have the disease.

Not wanting to end up in a nursing home, Roger and Theresa went to see an organization called Home Indeed about assistant living at home. The nurse running that organization told them that they would have a nurse come by and check on his condition but Theresa said to her, "Sooner or later, we'll need a live-in nurse to watch over Roger since now he has a tendency to wander off, especially at night." The nurse replied, "Yes, we do have a nurse who can do that. Her name is Ada Dickerson and she is a divorcee. Although she is only thirty-four, she was married twice but has no children. I will consult her and ask her if she is interested in the job. She is currently working at St. Jerome Hospital in nearby Rochester." The Hohlfeld's agreed and after agreeing a week later, Ada showed at Roger's house ready to assist him in any way possible. The agreement worked out fine. Gradually, Ada felt more and more like part of the family.

After talking to Hohlfeld, Barbara called Theresa to give her the grim news about her brother and the circumstances under which it happened. Theresa thought, 'Oh my God, I created a monster. All my life I tried to turn a blind eye to his actions but no more'. Then she told Barbara, "I'll come down to see you and Dennis and find out more about Al. First, I believe that your father has Alzheimer's disease as he has already showed signs of it. We'll consult his doctor for more tests. I'll put him in a nursing home until I get back." Two days later, after putting Roger in a nursing home in nearby Rochester, Theresa began her long drive to Quitman, Missouri where Dennis and Barbara lived.

The next day after Hohlfeld was interned in the hospital when two deputies showed up to check up on him, Dr. Toby Taylor, thirty-six, told them, "We did all we could do for him here and we're ready to release him into your custody but I strongly advise you to keep him on a suicide watch. Right now, he is severely depressed and wishes to die." So around 10:00 am they took Hohlfeld to the Gentry County jail and kept him on a suicide watch.

Later that day, around 4:30 pm, Judge Joseph Sweeney, fifty-seven, showed up at the county courthouse to arraign Hohlfeld after Hohlfeld consulted his attorney, Jerry Slocum. At the arraignment, Judge Sweeney asked Slocum, "How does your client plea, guilty or not guilty?" Slocum replied, "He wishes to plead no contest, your honor." Then Sweeney said, "Bring Hohlfeld to court on Thursday, August 24 next, at 10:00 am and I will have determined his sentence. Court adjourned."

On Tuesday, August 22, Theresa, Barbara and her husband Dennis Mercer showed at the jail to visit Hohlfeld. Hohlfeld said, "Thank you all for coming here to see me but all I want to do now is to simply die. As you can see, I had my eyes jabbed out and will never be able to see again. I hope they give me the death penalty but they won't. In fact, while I was in Ohio just before I came to Missouri, I killed a four-year-old girl by the name of Judy Thornburg. So, I plan to confess to that if there is a death penalty in Ohio." Theresa replied, "Please Al, don't talk like that. You'll eventually get used to being blind and life behind bars." Then Hohlfeld said, "I will receive my sentence around 10:00 am the day after tomorrow." Theresa replied, "We'll all be here. After you get out, you can always come to live with your father and I if we're still alive." Hohlfeld then said, "Thank you, Mom." Then Barbara said, "If not, then you can move in with Dennis and I. The girls will both be fully grown by then." Hohlfeld was moved by their statements but said, "I have no idea just how long I will be in prison." Theresa asked, "Al, do you know the _ who did this to you?" Hohlfeld replied, "No since they will not tell me her name." On their way out after visiting Hohlfeld, Theresa asked the desk sergeant, "Just who is the _ _ who blinded my son?" The desk sergeant relied, "Sorry Ma'am, we're not allowed to give out that information." Then Theresa replied yelling at the top of her lungs, "_ you, you_ _!" and left.

In the meantime, Hohlfeld contemplated confessing to killing Judy Thornburg in order to get the death penalty but because he was blind, he'll never get it so he decided against it.

At 10:00 am on Thursday, August 24, with Theresa, Barbara and Dennis present, Judge Sweeney took his seat at the bench and began reading Hohlfeld's sentence and said, "Hohlfeld, inasmuch as I feel sorry for you in your condition, I still have to punish you. I hereby sentence you to a term of not less than fifteen years nor more than twenty years to serve in the Missouri State Intermediate Security Penitentiary for men located in Moberly, Missouri. Pending your transfer to Moberly, you're remanded into custody. Court adjourned." Then Hohlfeld asked the judge, "Is there a death penalty in Ohio, your honor?" Judge Sweeney replied, "I'm not quite sure but I believe there is. Why did you ask?" Hohlfeld simply said, "Never mind." A week later on August 31, Hohlfeld was taken by two state marshals to Moberly.

As for Judy Schaan, after graduating from Stanberry High School in 1984, she enrolled at Missouri State College in Kansas City with a major in medicine. She graduated four years later and in 1989, she was hired as a registered nurse to work at the Green Hills Rehabilitation Center three miles east of Albany.

That weekend, Theresa left and drove back to her home in Sterling Heights, Michigan. Two days later after arriving home, Theresa drove to Rochester to pick up Roger. Roger's condition seems to have gotten worse. Finally, after it was confirmed that Roger did have the disease, Theresa hired Ada Dickerson to be with Roger.

After that, they went to consult a lawyer Adam Harris in Mt. Clemens in order to give Theresa power of attorney over their affairs such as their finances. Now having the power of attorney, Theresa decided to no longer bankroll Hohlfeld since he would no longer need it where he was but did send him cigarettes and candy. In the meantime, Hohlfeld signed over his 1974 Ford Mustang to Dennis.

Back in Michigan, Ada has a cousin by the name of David Jennings who was a psychologist and work for the Macomb County of Corrections in Mt. Clemens. His job was to determine whether a detainee was competent to stand trial or not and to classify them as to which part of jail they belonged. As he would sometimes visit Ada, he noticed Theresa's full figure. In fact, at sixty-four, Theresa never lost her voluptuous shape although her hair was turning grey. Although David married his high school sweetheart Sandra Kearns in 1974 after he received his degree in psychology, he continued seeing other women. They never had any children. While Ada was taking care of Roger, David, thirty-three, and Theresa began their affair.

www.ingramcontent.com/pod-product-compliance
Lightning Source LLC
Chambersburg PA
CBHW030826200726
48288CB00004B/1410

9781774191095